Lizard
loses his tail

Story by Beverley Randell
Illustrated by Bruce Lauchlan

Here is Lizard.

He is asleep in the sun.

Here is Kingfisher.

Kingfisher is hungry.

He is looking for a lizard.

Lizard wakes up.

Look!

Here comes Kingfisher.

Here comes Kingfisher.
Away goes Lizard.
Look at Lizard's tail!

Lizard is going home.

He is **safe**.

Where is Lizard's tail?

Kingfisher
is **eating**
Lizard's tail.